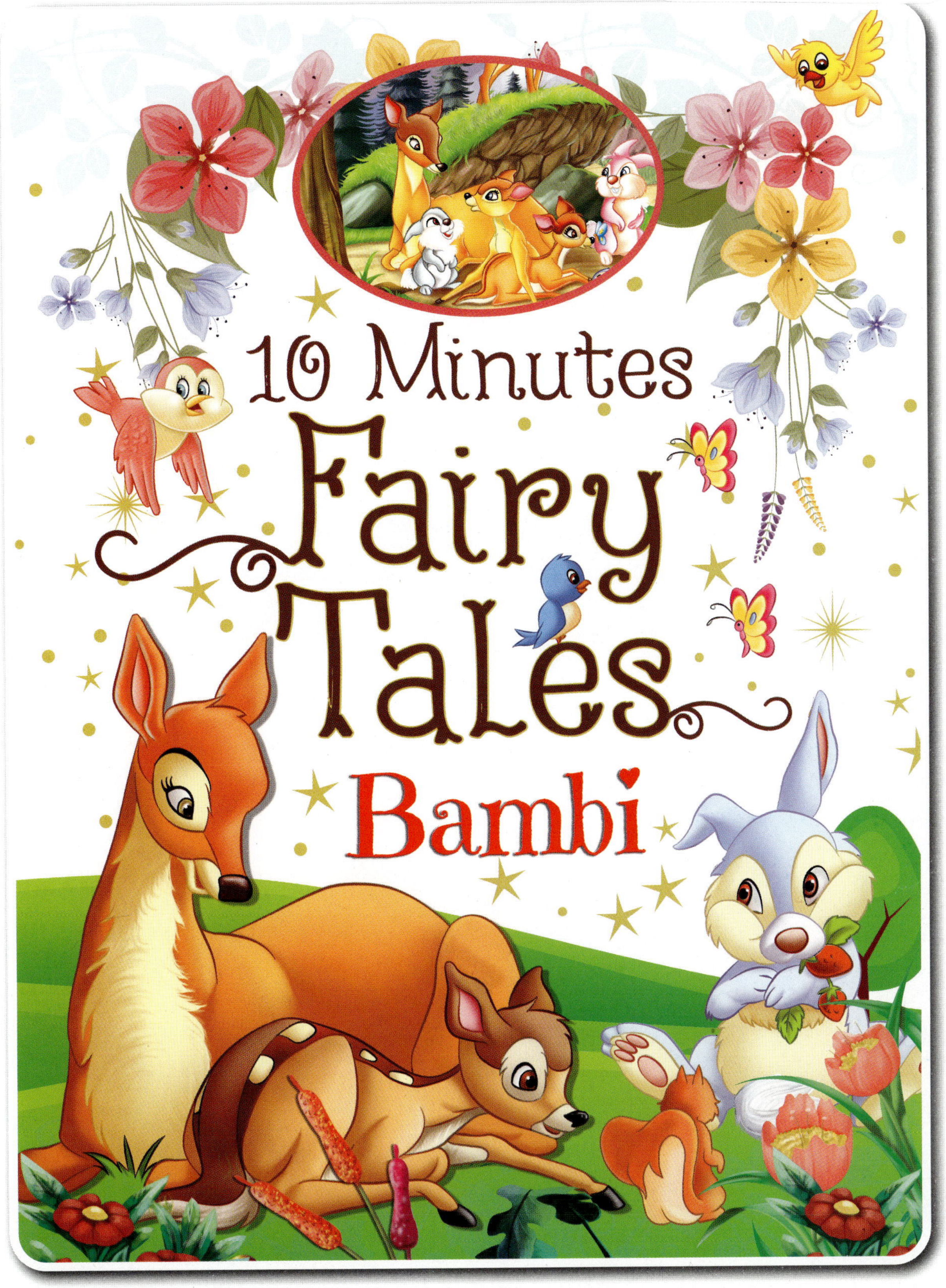

10 Minutes
Fairy Tales
Bambi

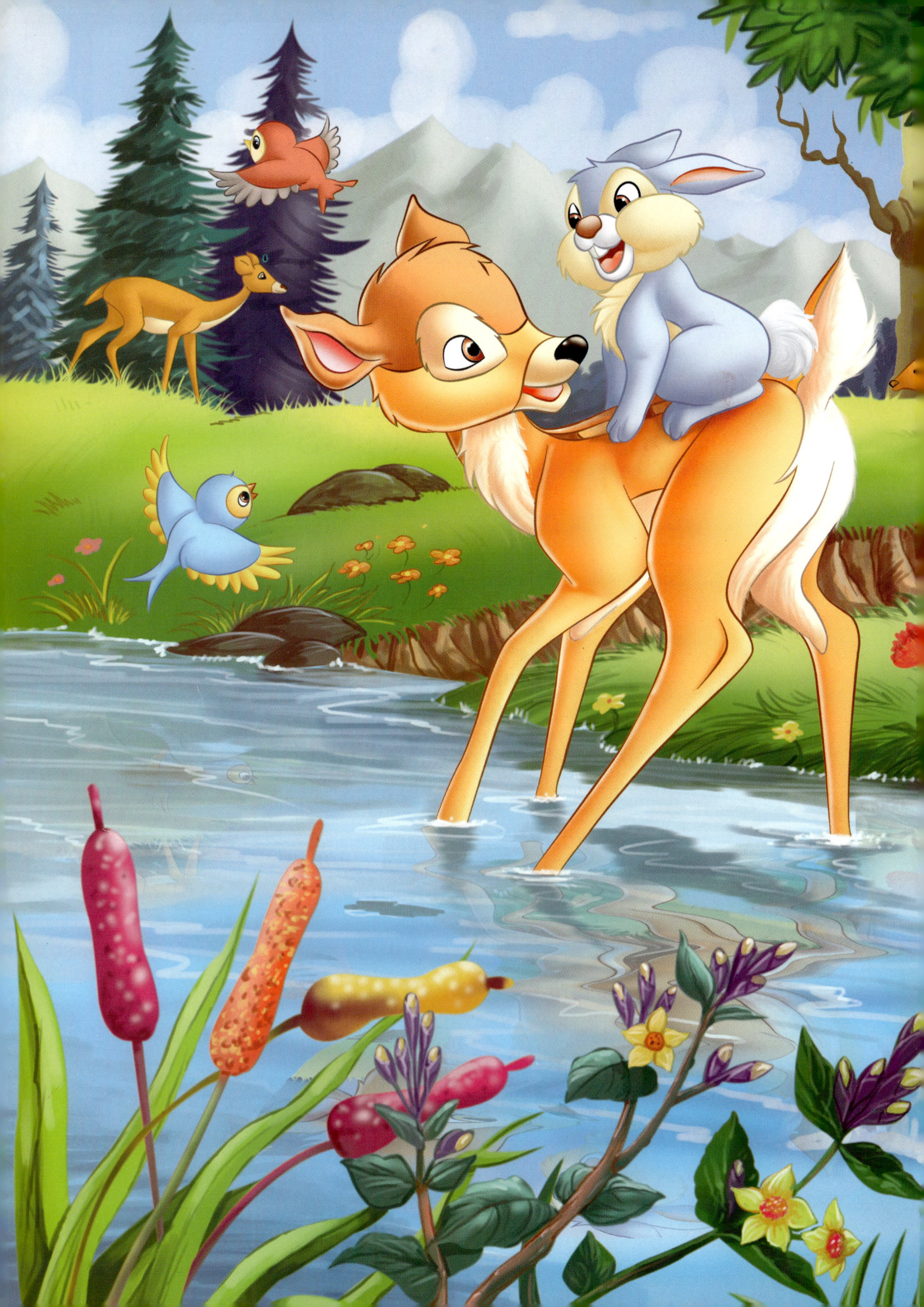

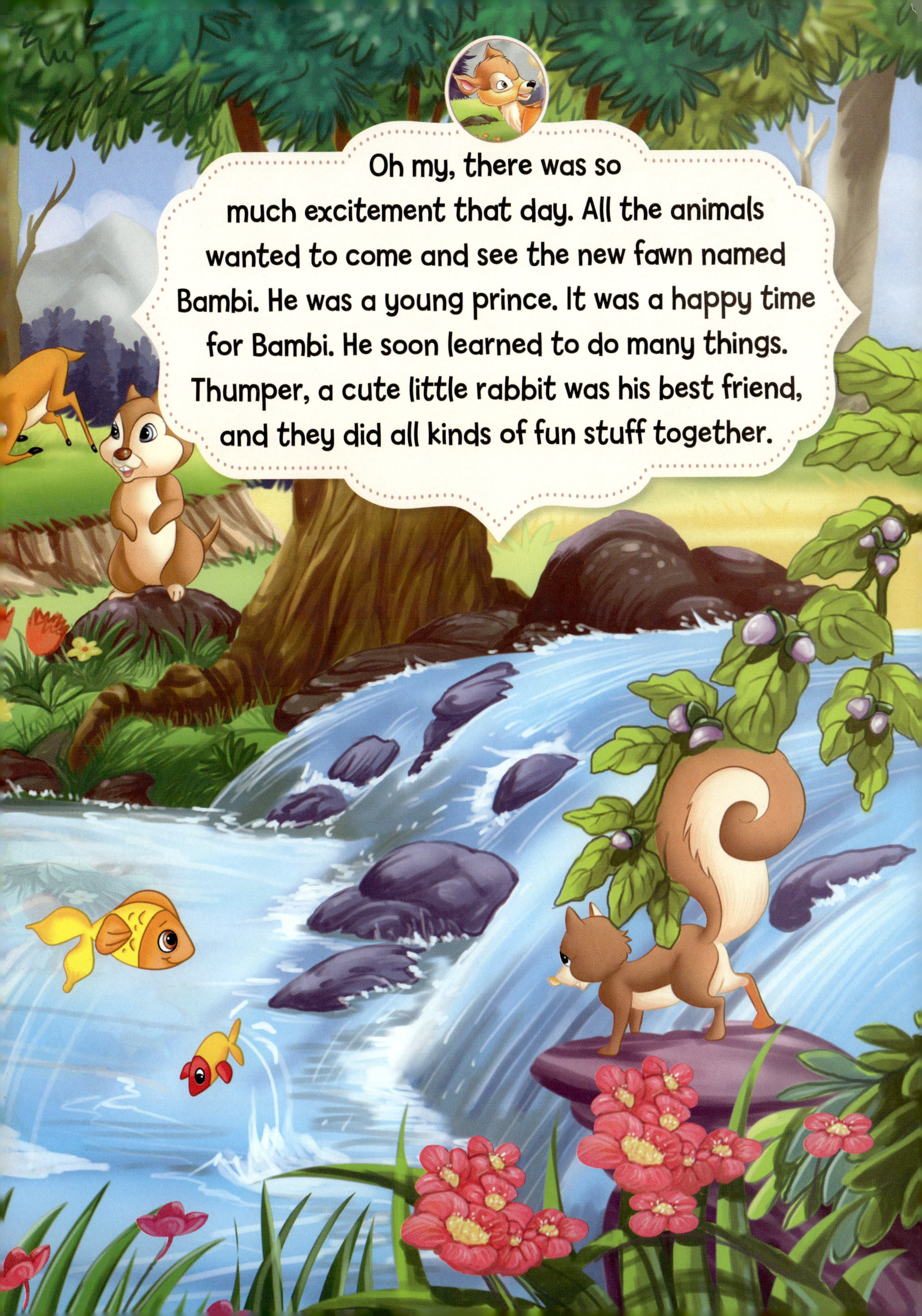

Oh my, there was so much excitement that day. All the animals wanted to come and see the new fawn named Bambi. He was a young prince. It was a happy time for Bambi. He soon learned to do many things. Thumper, a cute little rabbit was his best friend, and they did all kinds of fun stuff together.

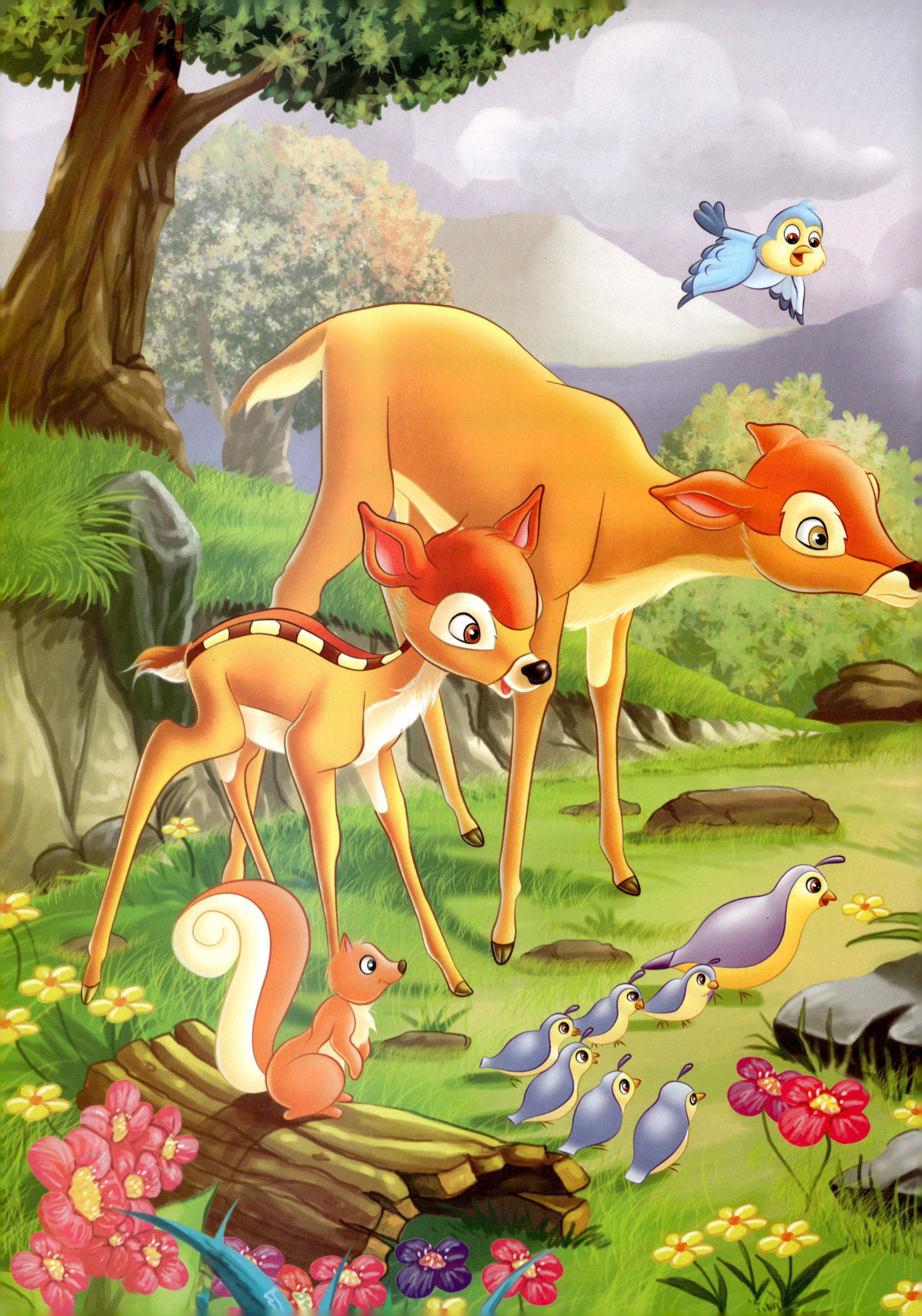

After playing for some time, Thumper, the rabbit, soon ran away to spread the news of the little fawn in the forest. Shortly, the rabbit was out of sight. Bambi was enjoying himself in his new home. “He looks so sweet,” said the quail, who happened to pass by Bambi.

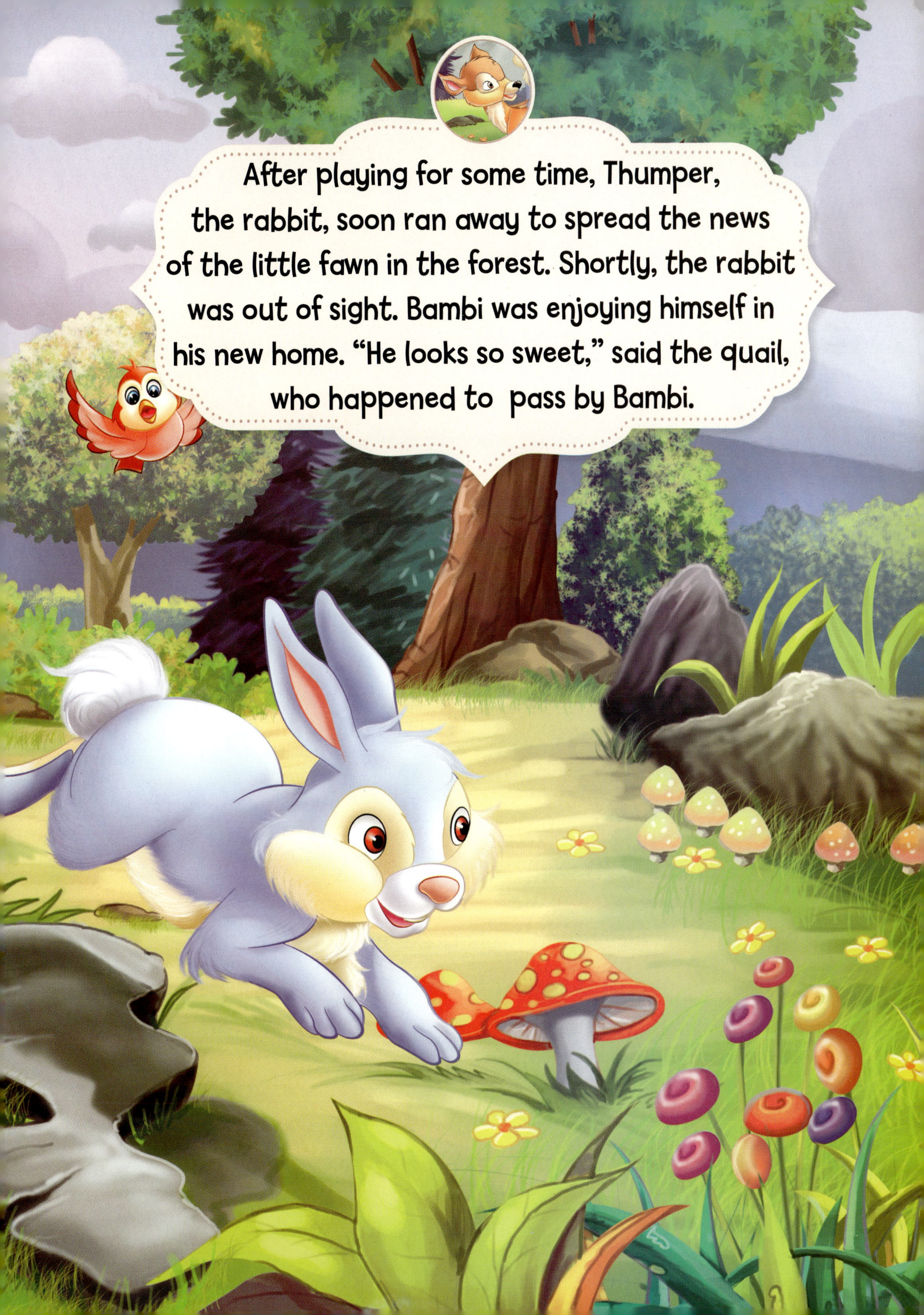

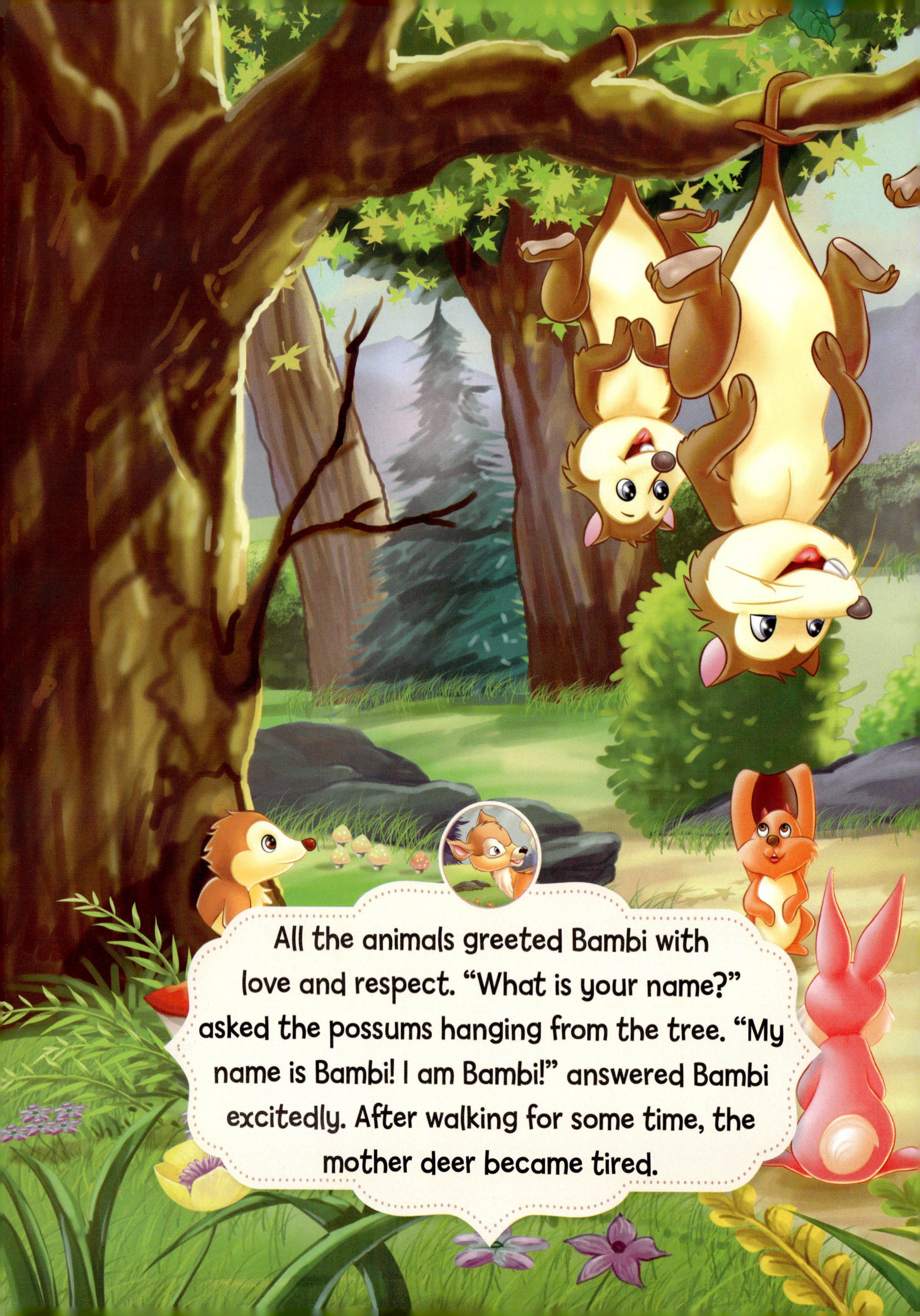

All the animals greeted Bambi with love and respect. “What is your name?” asked the possums hanging from the tree. “My name is Bambi! I am Bambi!” answered Bambi excitedly. After walking for some time, the mother deer became tired.

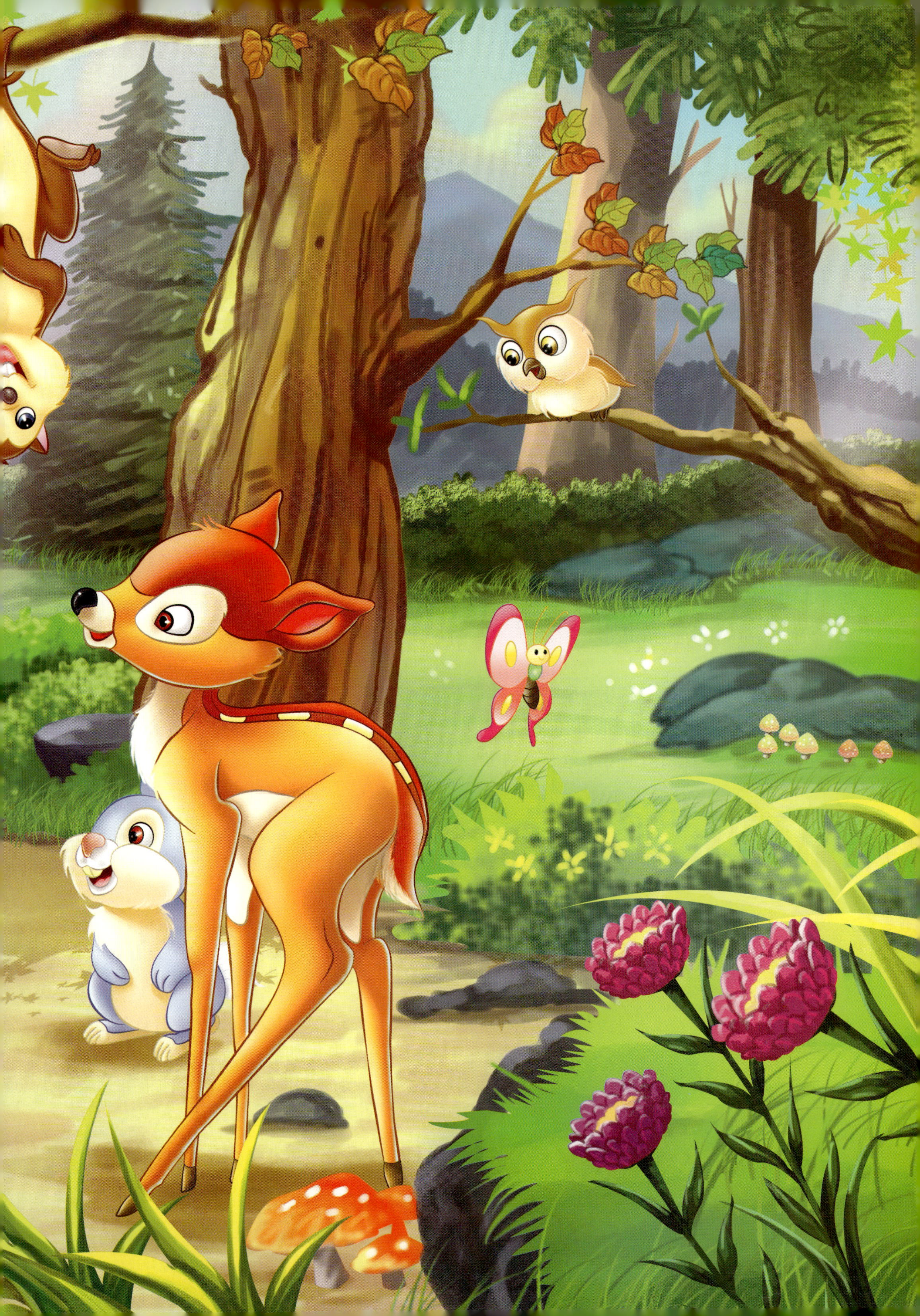

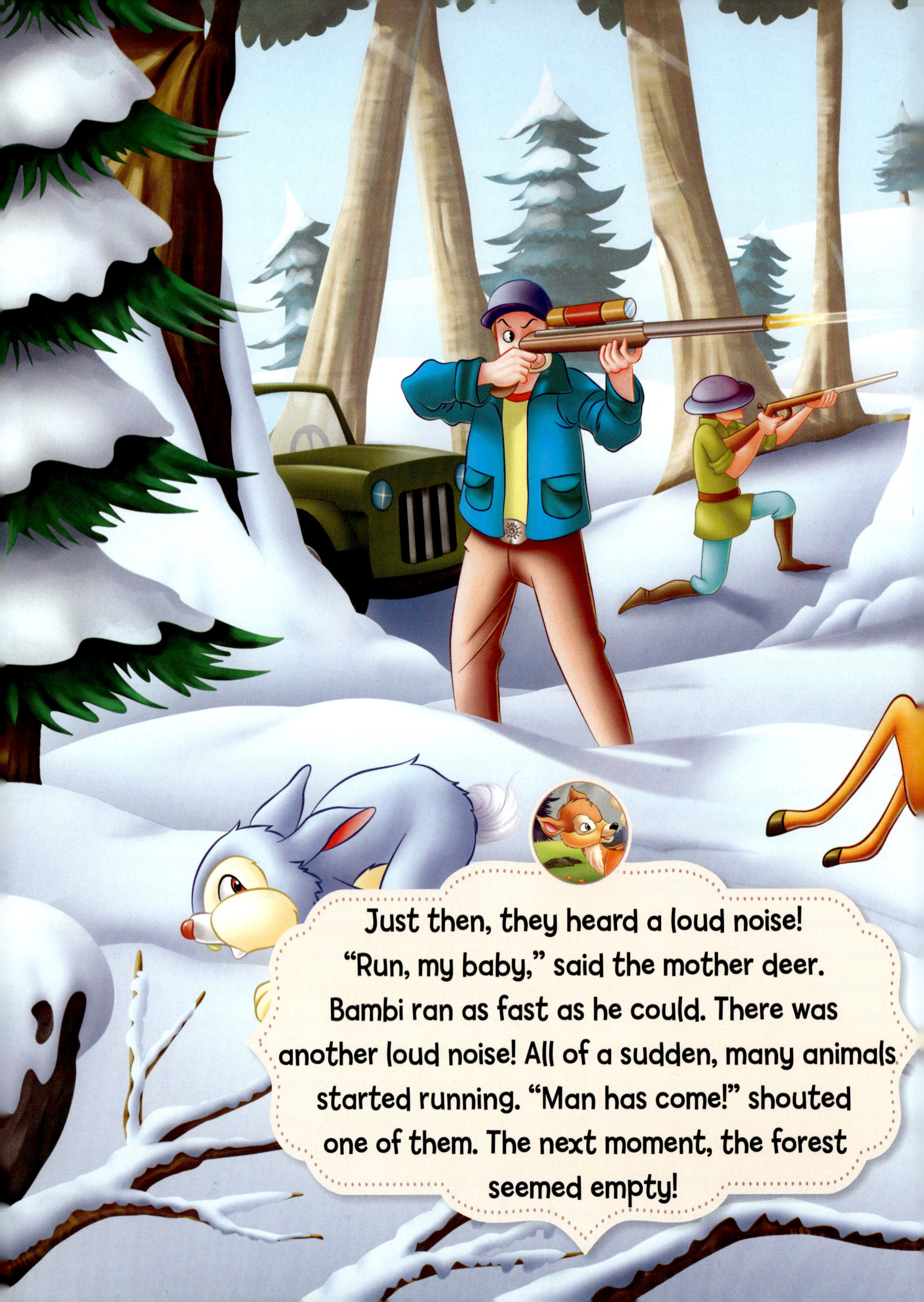

Just then, they heard a loud noise! "Run, my baby," said the mother deer. Bambi ran as fast as he could. There was another loud noise! All of a sudden, many animals started running. "Man has come!" shouted one of them. The next moment, the forest seemed empty!

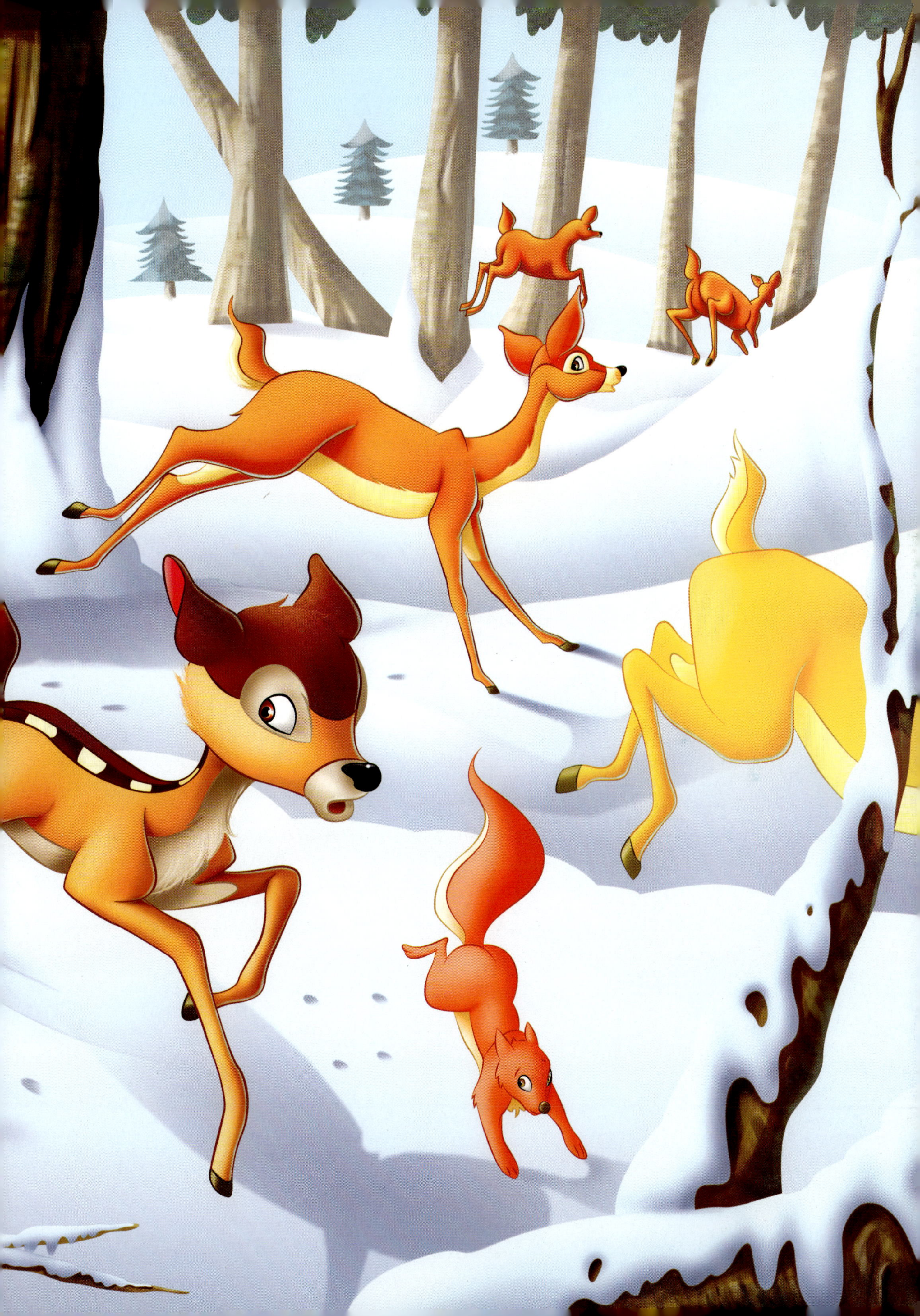

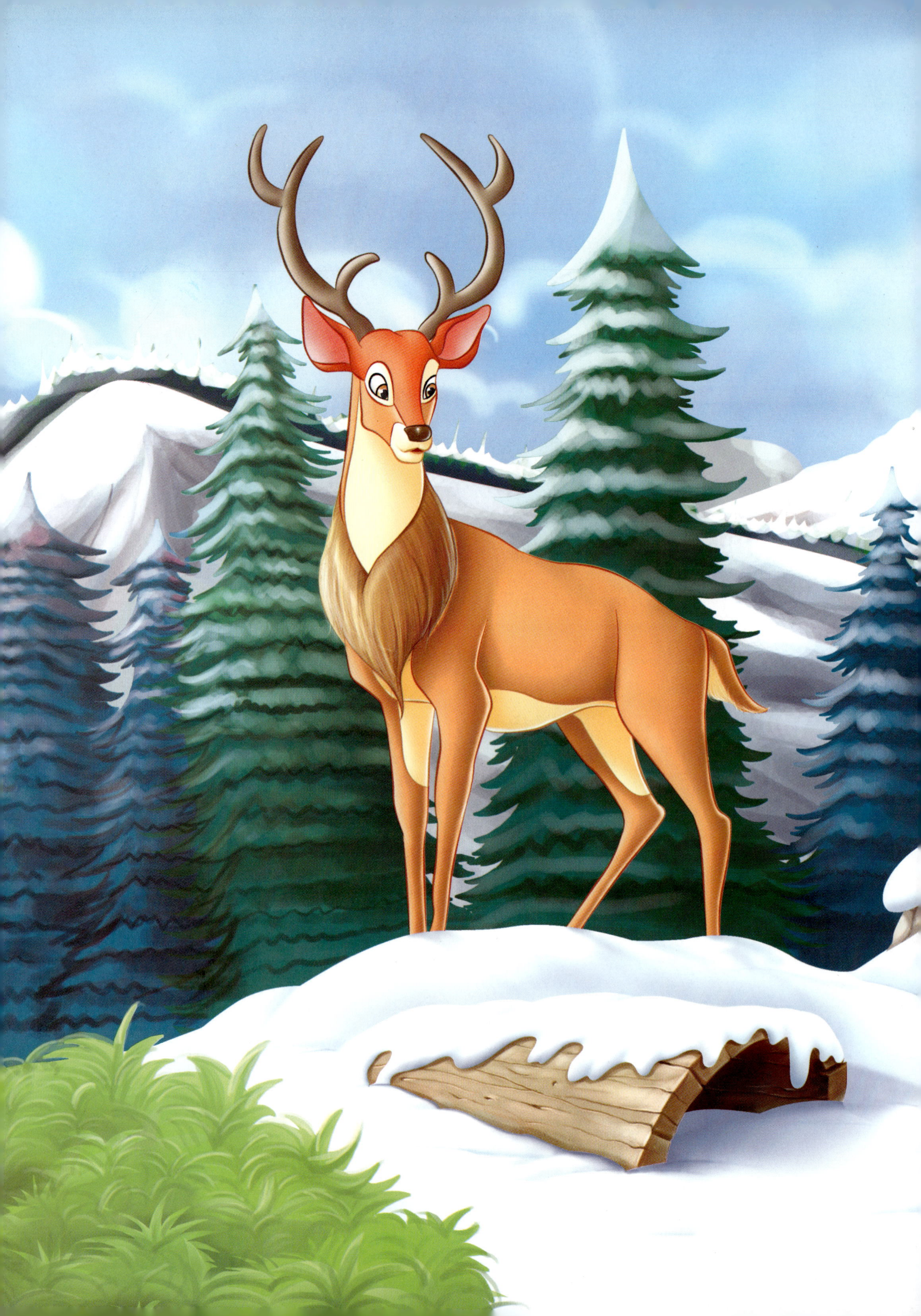

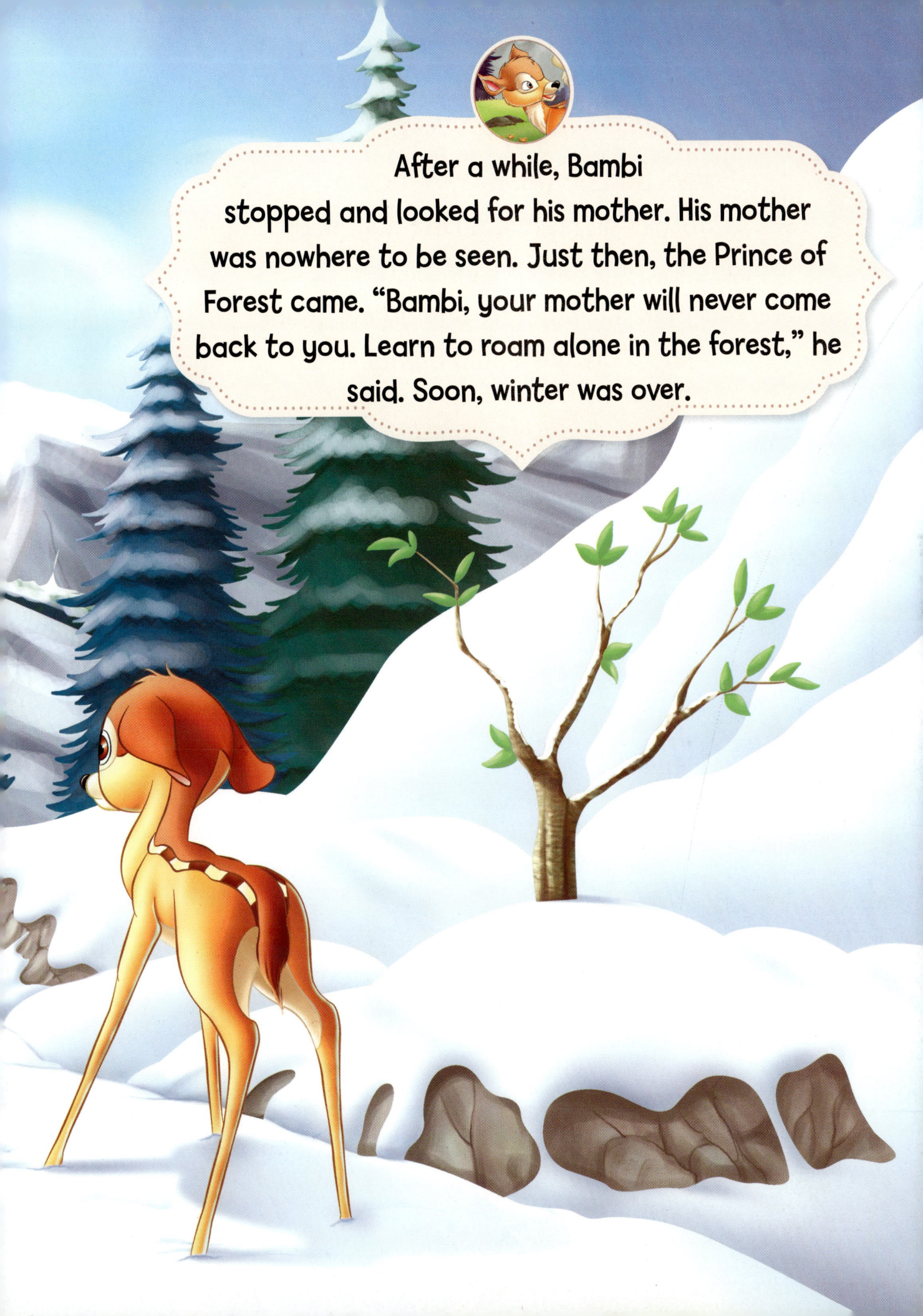

After a while, Bambi stopped and looked for his mother. His mother was nowhere to be seen. Just then, the Prince of Forest came. “Bambi, your mother will never come back to you. Learn to roam alone in the forest,” he said. Soon, winter was over.

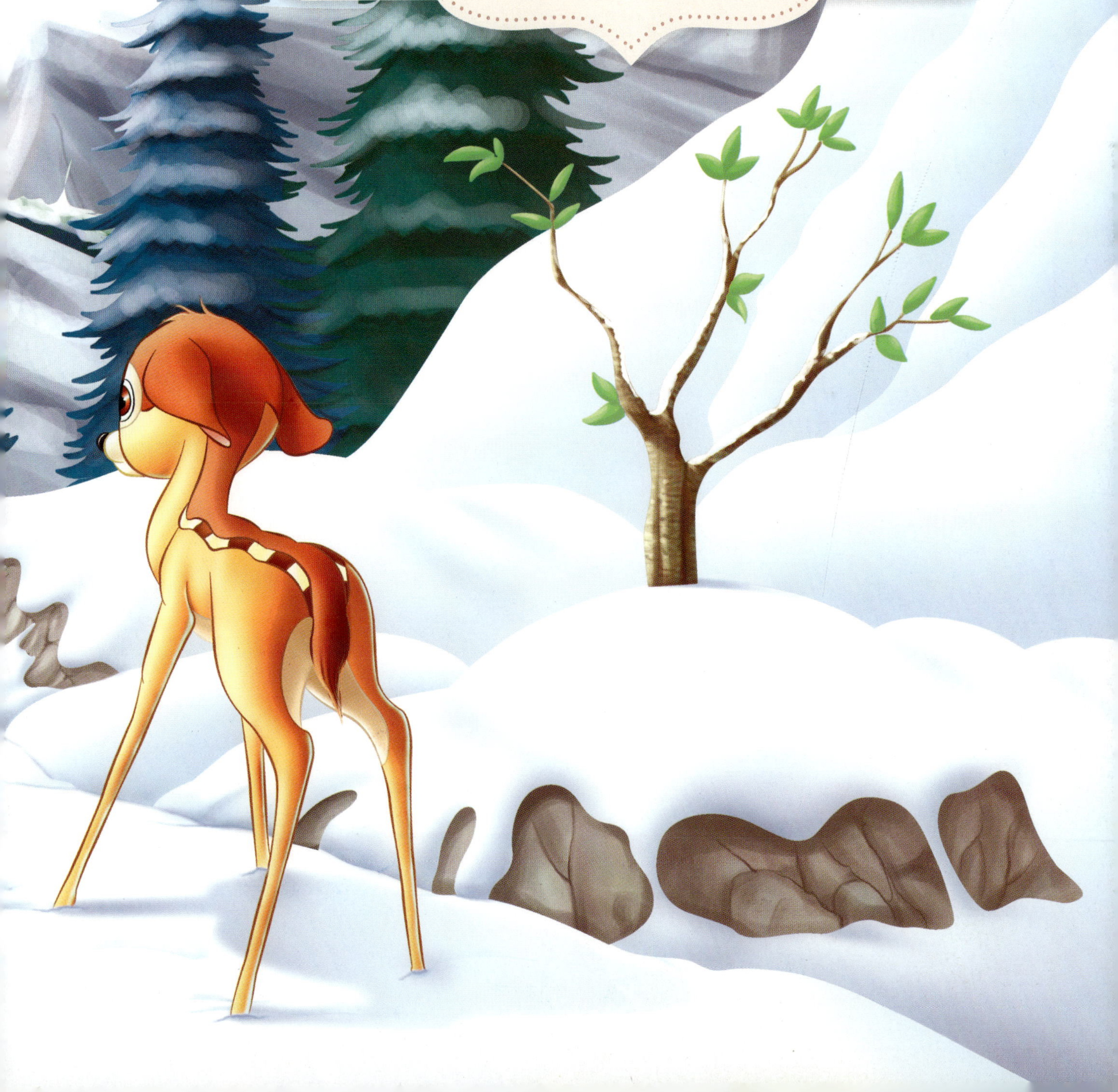

Bambi had grown. He now had a set of antlers on his head. One day, while walking in the forest, he met a doe. “Do you recognise me, Bambi?” she asked. “I am Alina. “Oh, yes!” said Bambi.

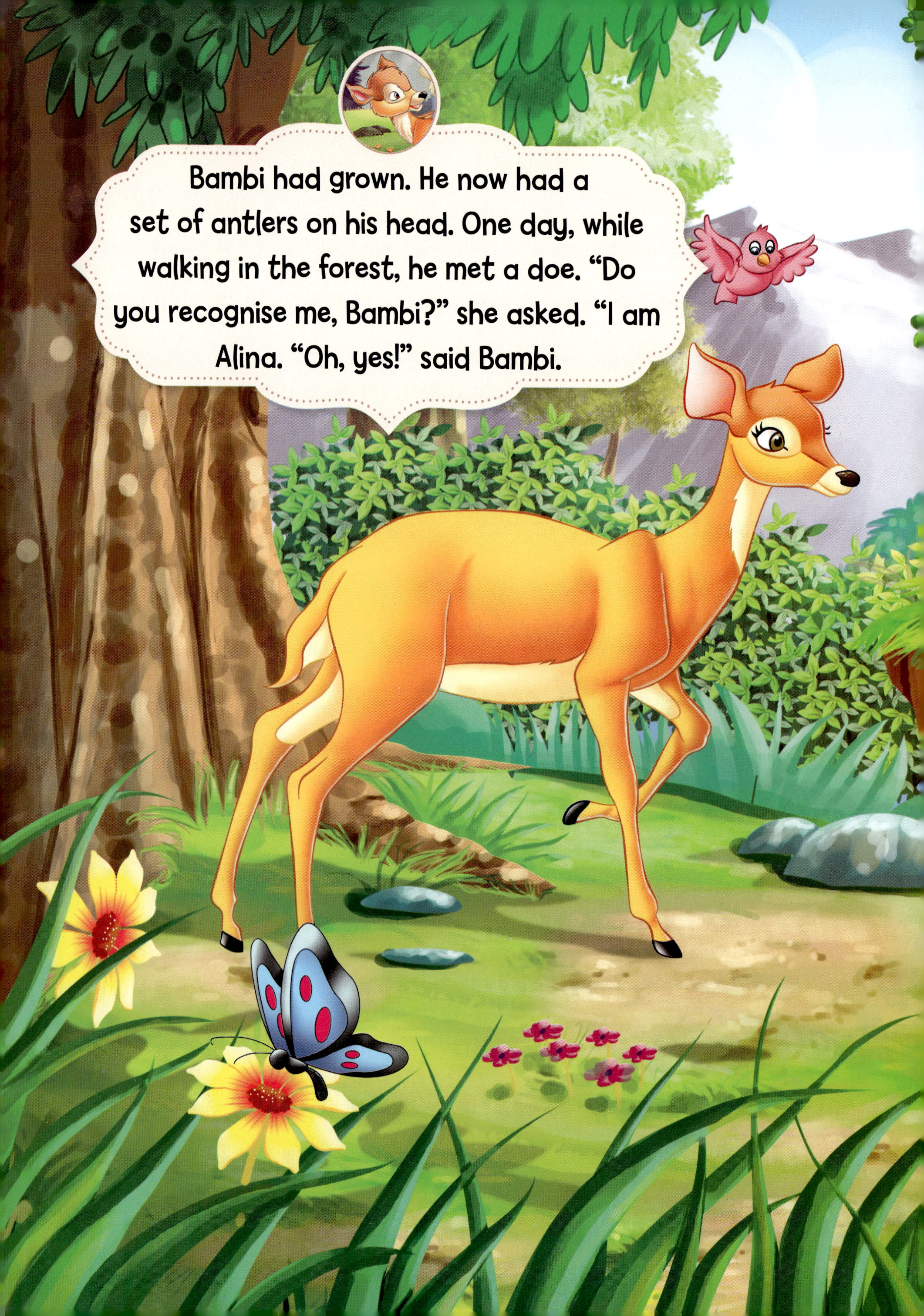

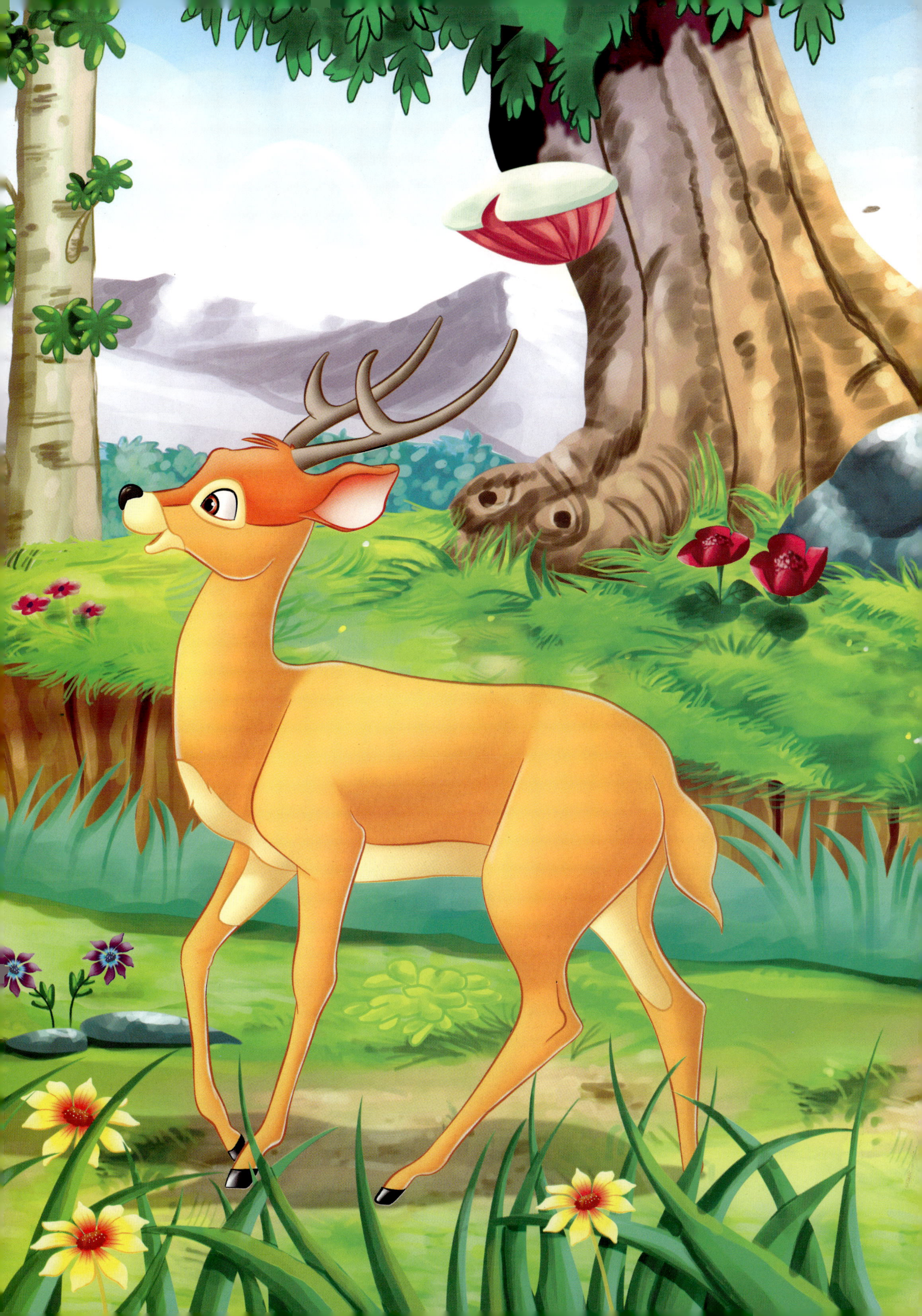

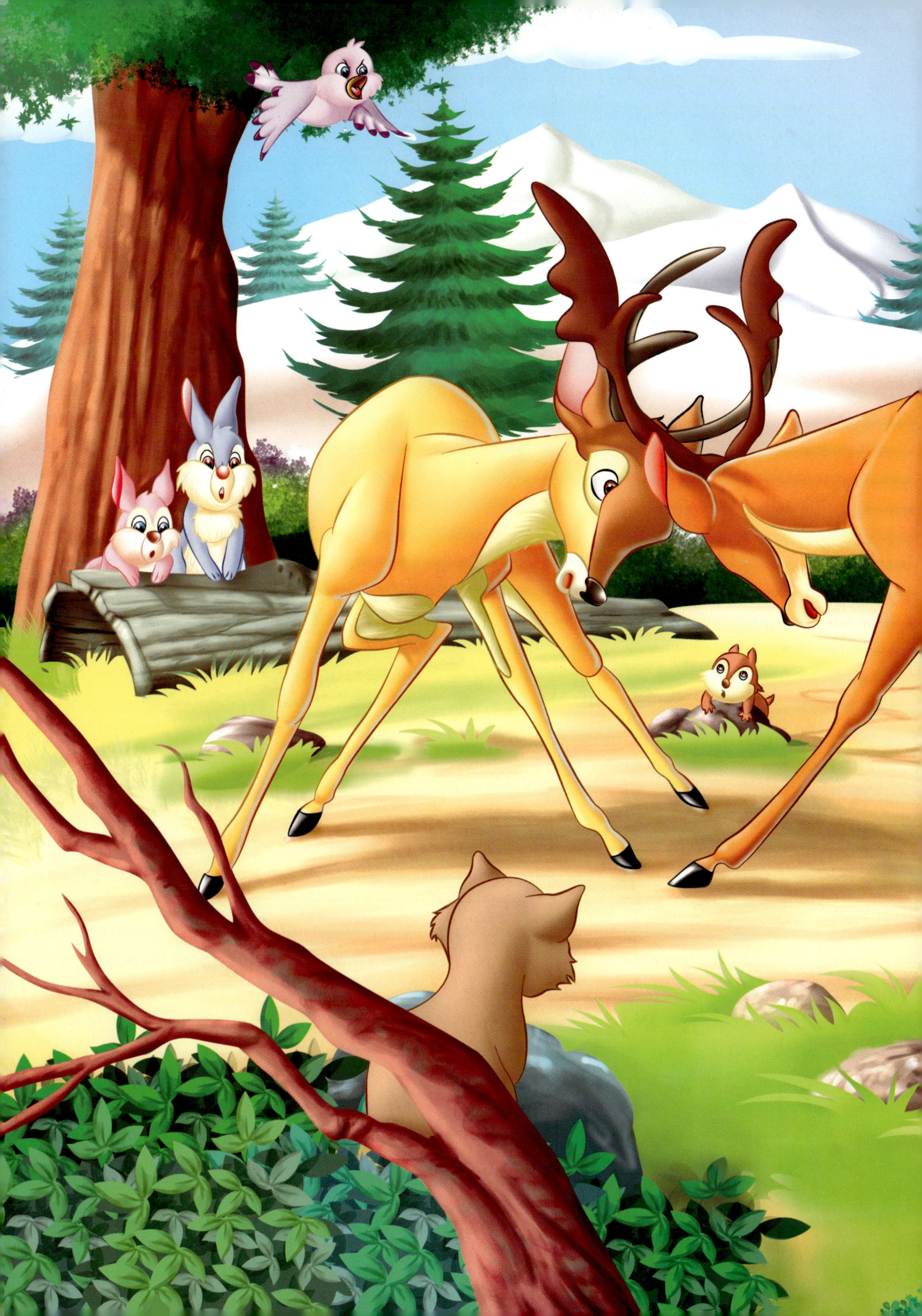

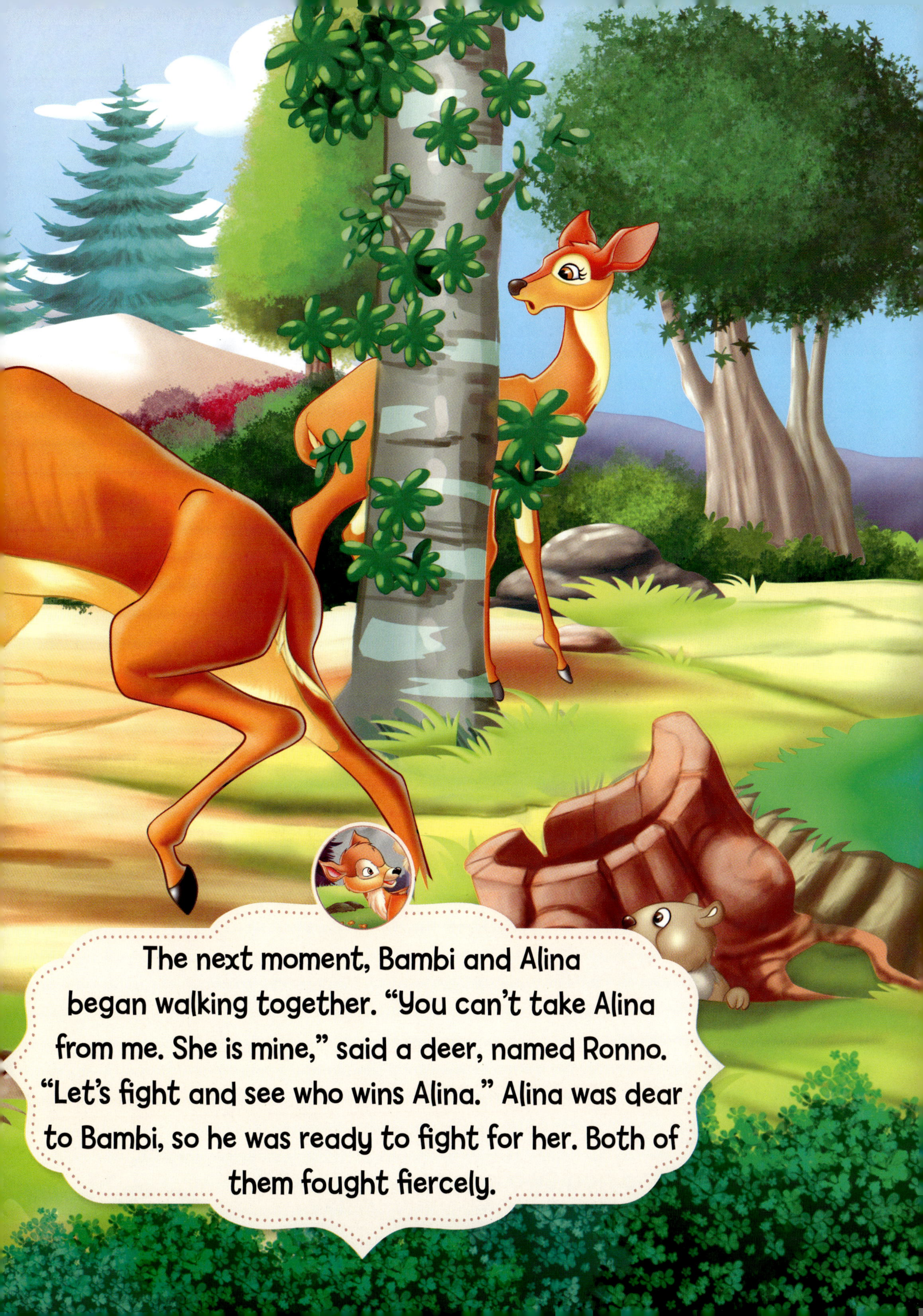

The next moment, Bambi and Alina began walking together. "You can't take Alina from me. She is mine," said a deer, named Ronno. "Let's fight and see who wins Alina." Alina was dear to Bambi, so he was ready to fight for her. Both of them fought fiercely.

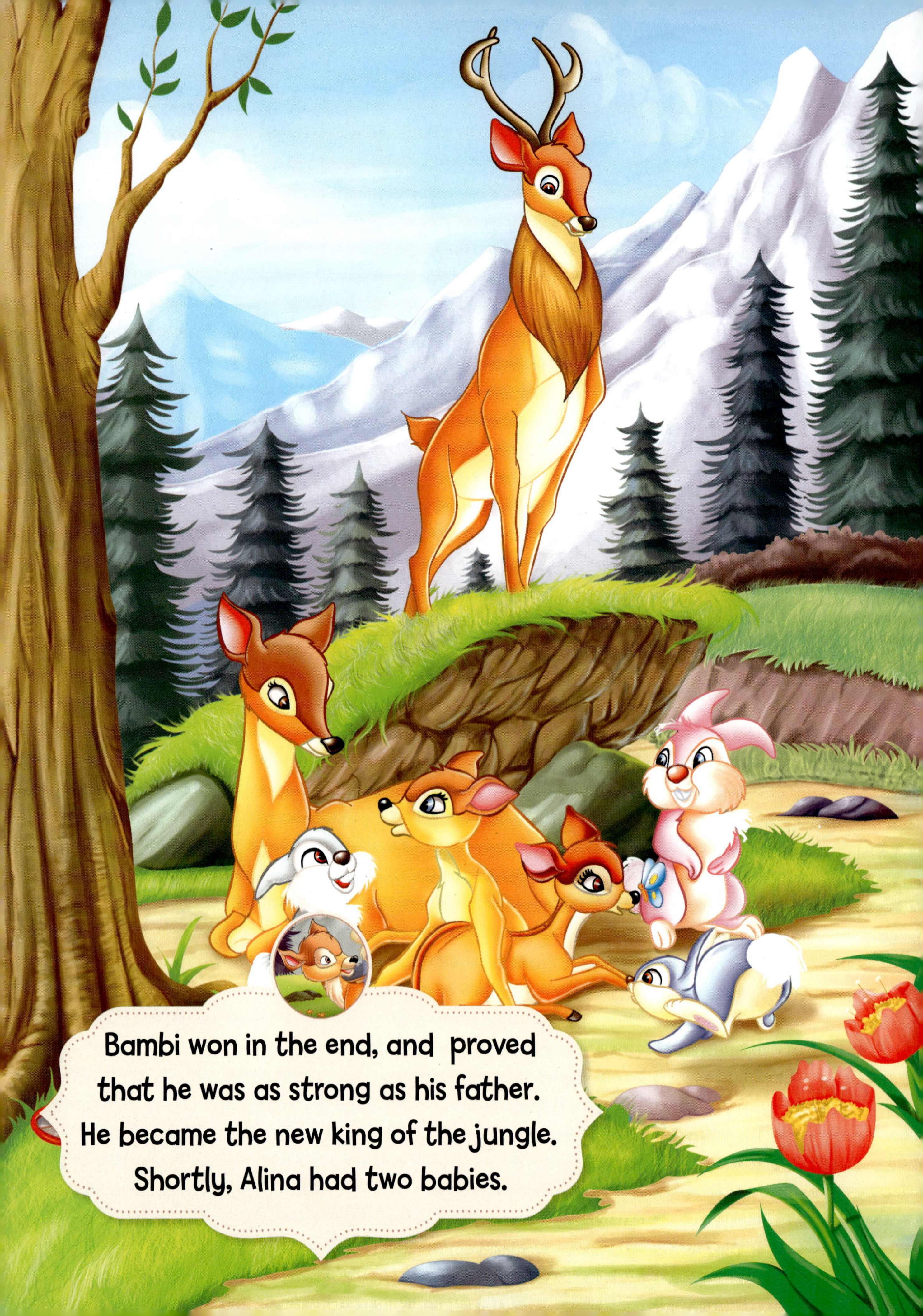

Bambi won in the end, and proved
that he was as strong as his father.
He became the new king of the jungle.
Shortly, Alina had two babies.